Chantrell Creek Elementary

Chantrell Creek Elementary

# THE WORLD OF
# FOOD

## Paula S. Wallace

**Gareth Stevens Publishing**
A WORLD ALMANAC EDUCATION GROUP COMPANY

Please visit our web site at: www.garethstevens.com
For a free color catalog describing Gareth Stevens Publishing's list of high-quality books
and multimedia programs, call 1-800-542-2595 (USA) or 1-800-387-3178 (Canada).
Gareth Stevens Publishing's fax: (414) 332-3567.

Library of Congress Cataloging-in-Publication Data

Wallace, Paula S.
    The world of food / by Paula S. Wallace.
        p. cm. — (Life around the world)
    Summary: Discusses foods that are popular in countries around the world and includes a recipe
from each country, including Australia, Brazil, Egypt, Germany, India, Japan, Mexico, Russia,
South Africa, and the United States.
    Includes bibliographical references and index.
    ISBN 0-8368-3660-X (lib. bdg.)
    1. Cookery, International—Juvenile literature. [1. Food. 2. Cookery, International.] I. Title.
TX725.A1W293    2003
641.59—dc21                                                    2002036654

First published in 2003 by
**Gareth Stevens Publishing**
A World Almanac Education Group Company
330 West Olive Street, Suite 100
Milwaukee, Wisconsin 53212 USA

Produced by Design Press, a division of the Savannah College of Art and Design.
Designers: Janice Shay, Maria Angela Rojas, Andrea Messina.
Editors/Researchers: Gwen Strauss, Nancy Axelrad, Lisa Bahlinger, Martha G.
 Nesbitt, Susan Smits, Cameron Spencer, Elizabeth Hudson-Goff.

Gareth Stevens editor: Dorothy L. Gibbs
Gareth Stevens designer: Tammy Gruenewald

Photo Credits
Corbis: page 15; /Staffan Widstrand, page 7; /Ariel Skelley, cover, page 19;
 /David Turnley, cover, page 31; /Dean Conger, page 35.
Getty Images: /David Frazier, page 11; /Nicholas DeVore, page 23; /V.C.L., page 39;
 /SW Productions, cover, page 43.
Picture Quest: /Corbis Images, page 26 (bottom).
SuperStock: /Yoshio Tomii, page 27; /D. C. Lowe, page 30 (bottom); /Ben Mangor, page 38.
Additional photography by Campus Photography, Savannah College of Art and Design.

Illustration Credits
Andrea Messina: page 34.
Hui-Mei Pan: pages 6, 10, 13, 14, 28, 29, 36, 41, 42.

Printed in the United States of America

1 2 3 4 5 6 7 8 9 07 06 05 04 03

# CONTENTS

Words that appear in the glossary are printed in
**boldface** type the first time they occur in the text.

# Kitchen Safety Rules

1. Always ask permission before you cook anything.

2. Make sure a grown-up is present to help you.

3. Wash your hands before you handle food and *always* after handling eggs or raw meat.

4. Before you start, read through the entire recipe and gather all the utensils and ingredients you will need.

5. Never touch hot pots, pans, or baking sheets or hot liquids, especially hot oil.

6. Pin back long hair and don't wear loose, baggy clothing that could catch fire.

7. Never use a sharp knife without a grown-up to help you and always use a cutting board.

8. Make sure your hands are dry when you use electric appliances and never use electric appliances near water.

All over the world, people's tastes are as much the same as they are different. Children and grown-ups everywhere have favorite foods and traditional meals from their own regions, but they also enjoy foods from many other places throughout the world. Some foods of other countries might seem strange to you, but discovering new tastes and new ways to prepare foods can be fun.

Cooking is a great way to learn about the traditions and tastes of other countries. The recipes in this book can help you discover the fun of creating meals and snacks from around the world. Special activities are also included to help you understand the cultures of the countries featured. The recipes and activities in this book are easy to do, but children should always have a grown-up helping them in the kitchen. Children need help using sharp knives and electric appliances, such as food processors and blenders, and a grown-up should always turn on the stove or oven and handle hot foods and hot cookware and utensils.

Wherever you're from, one thing is sure, families and friends get enjoyment and pleasure from preparing and sharing meals together.

---

 **Note:** *Whenever you see this sign, you must ask a grown-up for help.*

 **Note:** *Whenever you see this sign, you will need to use a photocopy machine.*

# AUSTRALIA

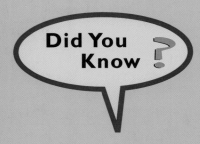

Because Australia was **colonized** by people from England, most Australians speak British English or a kind of English that is full of Australian **slang**. How would you answer if someone asked if you would like a *bicky*? Or a *lolly*? Some *chook*? Or some other kind of *tucker*? *Aussie* children enjoy a *sanger* for lunch or an Aussie meat pie with *chips*. Most Australian homes have *barbies,* so eating meals outdoors is very popular. Aussies share the English tradition of afternoon tea, which is usually a snack of sangers and bickies with tea or juice to drink. For thousands of years, the **Aborigines** (a-boh-RIJ-en-eez) have dined on bush tucker, which means the plants, birds, reptiles, and insects from the bush, or wilderness region. Witchetty **grub** is a popular bush tucker treat. It is a white worm that is eaten alive or cooked and tastes like almonds.

## Aussie Strine

| | | |
|---|---|---|
| *Aussie* . . . Australian | *chips* . . . . french fries | *sanger* . . . sandwich |
| *barbie* . . . barbecue | *chook* . . . chicken | *strine* . . . slang |
| *bicky* . . . . biscuit or cookie | *lolly* . . . . . candy | *tucker* . . . food |

# How to make

## Anzac* Biscuits

### Ingredients:

| | |
|---|---|
| vegetable cooking spray | 1 teaspoon baking soda |
| 1 cup (80 grams) shredded coconut | pinch of salt |
| 1 cup (100 g) rolled oats | $\frac{1}{2}$ cup (110 g) or 1 stick butter or margarine |
| 1 cup (150 g) flour | 2 tablespoons molasses |
| 1 cup (220 g) sugar | 2 tablespoons water |

**You will need:**
• baking sheet
• measuring cups and spoons
• large mixing bowl
• wooden spoon
• small saucepan
• fork
• **spatula**

Spray a baking sheet with vegetable cooking spray. Heat oven to 350° Fahrenheit (175° Celsius). Put coconut, rolled oats, flour, sugar, baking soda, and salt in a large mixing bowl. Stir with a wooden spoon. Melt butter or margarine in a small saucepan over low heat. Stir in molasses and water. Pour the liquid mixture into the flour mixture and blend well with a wooden spoon. Drop teaspoonfuls of dough onto the baking sheet, about 2 inches (5 centimeters) apart. Press down each blob of dough with a fork. Bake 12 to 15 minutes, until biscuits are golden brown. Use a spatula to take the biscuits off of the baking sheet. Let the biscuits cool for at least 10 minutes before serving them. (Makes about 30 biscuits.)

Because of **rationing**, eggs were not easy to find during World War II. Australians created eggless biscuits (cookies) to send to their troops. These biscuits were soon being called ANZACs, which is short for Australian and New Zealand Army Corps.

# How to make Grub Tucker

**You will need:**
- chocolate cookies
- self-sealing plastic bag
- rolling pin
- new flowerpot
- gummy worms

Put chocolate cookies into a self-sealing plastic bag. Crush the cookies with a rolling pin until they look like dirt. Thoroughly wash and dry a new, unused flowerpot. Pour the cookie "dirt" into the flowerpot. Arrange the gummy worms so they look like they are crawling out of the dirt. Dig in!

# BRAZIL

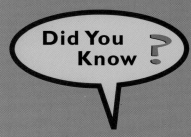

*Amazon* is the name of the world's largest river. It is also the name of the large rain forest around the river. The world's largest snake, the anaconda (an-uh-KON-duh), lives in the Amazon. This snake can grow up to 30 feet (9 meters) long and can open its mouth wide enough to swallow a deer.

Because of its location near the **equator**, Brazil is a country full of tropical fruits. Thirsty Brazilians drink lots of fresh fruit juices.

The country's colorful mixture of cultures makes Brazilian cooking special. The national **cuisine** is a blend of Portuguese, native Indian, and African flavors. Carnival celebrations in Brazil are always a festive mix of food and music.

Lunch is the main meal of the day. At noon, the temperature is very hot, so after lunch, people take a break. They rest and wait for the day to cool down before returning to work or school.

Brazilians are very polite and careful about their table manners. It is bad manners in Brazil to eat while walking or riding. Also, Brazilians do not touch food with their fingers. Forks and knives are used even for eating sandwiches, pizza, and *pão de queijo* (PAH-oh jee KAY-joo), which is a favorite snack food.

## Tasty Spider

The Goliath bird-eating spider of the Amazon is a tarantula as big as a dinner plate. Some Amazonians, in fact, eat it for dinner! They wrap the spider in leaves and cook it over an open fire.

# How to make Pão de Queijo*

**You will need:**
- baking sheet
- measuring cups and spoons
- large mixing bowl
- microwave-safe glass bowl
- wooden spoon

**Ingredients:**

vegetable cooking spray

2 cups (360 g) tapioca flour*

²/₃ cup (160 milliliters) vegetable oil

¹/₃ cup (80 ml) water

1 teaspoon salt

2 eggs

6 ounces (170 g) grated parmesan cheese

 Spray a baking sheet with vegetable cooking spray. Heat oven to 375° F (190° C). Put the tapioca flour in a large mixing bowl and set aside. Combine the vegetable oil, water, and salt in a microwave-safe glass bowl. Heat the liquid mixture in a microwave oven for 1 minute, or until white foam appears on the top. Have a grown-up pour the hot liquid into the bowl of tapioca flour. Mix with a wooden spoon, then let the dough rest for 10 minutes. Mix in the eggs and cheese. Taking a teaspoonful of dough at a time, roll the dough between your hands to form a ball. Place the balls on the baking sheet, 1 inch (2.5 cm) apart. Bake 20 to 25 minutes, until the tops of the balls begin to turn brown. (Makes about 24 cheese balls.)

 These easy and fun-to-make cheese balls come from Minas (MEE-nahs), which is a state in Brazil that is famous for its cooking. Tapioca flour, which is also called cassava flour, is available at health food stores and some supermarkets.

# How to make a **Rain Stick**

**You will need:**
- 70 or more flat-headed nails
- cardboard tube about 12 inches (30 cm) long and 2 inches (5 cm) around
- masking tape or strapping tape
- thick cardboard
- scissors
- paper
- glue
- acrylic paint or poster paint
- paintbrushes

**❶** Push 40 nails into the sides of the cardboard tube at different points down the whole length of the tube and all the way around the tube.

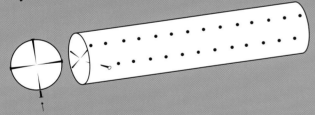

**❷** Cover one end of the tube with several layers of masking tape or strapping tape.

**❸** Fill the tube with at least 30 nails. Then, holding thick cardboard over the open end, tilt the tube back and forth to see if you like the sound.

**❹** Change the number of nails or try some other fillings, such as corn, beans, or rice, to get a sound you like. Then cover the open end of the tube with tape.

**❺** Cut paper to fit around the tube and glue the paper in place. Then paint and decorate your rain stick.

**About 10 percent of all animals and plants in the world live in the Amazon rain forest. A rain stick brings alive the sounds of the forest, reminding us how important it is to life on Earth.**

# EGYPT

Did You Know **?**

Ancient Egyptians cooked their meals on rooftops! Preparing food on top of their houses helped keep the houses cooler inside.

In ancient Egypt, sand would often get mixed in with the flour when people made bread, so eating too much bread would wear people's teeth down to the roots. Today, cooking methods in Egypt are much better, and Egyptian cuisine includes many delicious breads.

Bread is eaten at every meal in Egypt. Egyptian children enjoy a kind of flat, round bread called pita (PEE-tah). For lunch, they often eat their pita with hummus (HUH-miss), which is a spread made of mashed **chickpeas** and sesame butter. They also like to open the pita like a pocket and stuff it with falafel (fah-LAH-fuhl), which are crispy patties made of mashed chickpeas and herbs.

*Kebabs* (kuh-BOBS) are another popular food in Egypt. They are cubes of meat that are **skewered** on a stick with vegetables and grilled over a fire. Street stands in Egypt sell many kinds of food for snacking, as well as juice drinks made from limes, tangerines, and guavas.

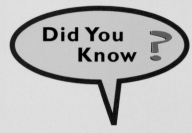

# How to make **Hummus**

**Ingredients:**

15 ounces (420 g) canned chickpeas, rinsed and drained

2 garlic cloves, crushed

3 tablespoons lemon juice

3 tablespoons tahini*

1 teaspoon salt

dash of paprika

**You will need:**
- can opener
- measuring spoons
- food processor

 Put all of the ingredients in a food processor and blend them until the mixture has a smooth, creamy texture. Use yummy hummus as a dip for vegetables or spread it on toasted pita.

**Toasted Pita:** With a small (and clean!) paintbrush, brush some olive oil on round pita bread. Toast the pita in the oven for a few minutes. A pizza cutter is a good way to slice toasted pita. You can cut the circle into triangles like you would cut a pizza or a pie.

**Vegetable Funny Faces:** Spread hummus on round pita bread. Add thin slices of carrots or red peppers for hair, whole cherry tomatoes or carrot slices for eyes, a black olive or half of a cherry tomato for a nose, and a curved stick of celery or a slice of a black olive for a mouth.

 Tahini (tah-HEE-nee) is a kind of butter made by crushing and mashing sesame seeds. You can find tahini at health food stores, and many grocery stores sell it in the international foods section.

# GERMANY

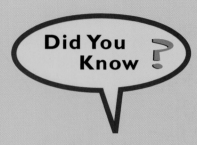

**Did You Know?**

Frankfurters (**FRAHNK**-fur-terz), or hotdogs, come from Frankfurt, Germany. A German might eat one on a roll with mustard for a morning snack.

For German children, the best time of year for eating is Christmastime, when the air is filled with the smells of cinnamon, cloves, roasting almonds, and baking cookies and gingerbread. The German town of Luebeck has a six-hundred-year-old tradition of making gingerbread called *lebkuchen* (LAYB-kook-hen), cinnamon star cookies called *zimsterne* (TZIM-shtair-nah), and candy known as marzipan (MAR-zee-pahn). Made of almond paste, marzipan is shaped and colored to look like fruit, flowers, and animals. Some marzipan makers are so good at sculpting fruit that people can't tell the difference between a marzipan apple and the real thing!

Of course, sweets are not the only foods Germans eat. They also like meat and potatoes, chicken and **dumplings**, noodles called *spätzle* (SHPET-sluh), cabbage, deviled eggs, and dill pickles. And Germans love freshly baked bread! Germany has three hundred kinds of bread and over a thousand different biscuits and cakes. Sausages, which Germans call "wursts," are also popular in Germany, where a sausage festival has been held every September for six hundred years.

# How to make **Spicy Stars**

**You will need:**
- mixing bowls
- sifter
- measuring cups and spoons
- electric mixer
- plastic wrap
- rolling pin
- star cookie cutters
- baking sheet

**Ingredients:**

3 cups (450 g) flour

$^1/_2$ teaspoon baking soda

$^1/_4$ teaspoon baking powder

$^1/_2$ cup (110 g) butter

$^1/_2$ cup (125 g) dark brown sugar, packed

2 teaspoons ground ginger

2 teaspoons ground cinnamon

pinch of ground cloves

1 teaspoon salt

1 teaspoon ground pepper

2 small eggs

$^1/_2$ cup (120 ml) molasses

extra flour

icing and sprinkles

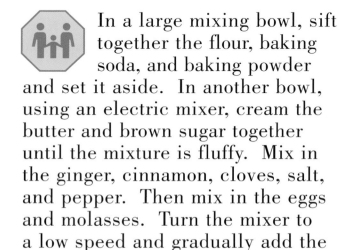

In a large mixing bowl, sift together the flour, baking soda, and baking powder and set it aside. In another bowl, using an electric mixer, cream the butter and brown sugar together until the mixture is fluffy. Mix in the ginger, cinnamon, cloves, salt, and pepper. Then mix in the eggs and molasses. Turn the mixer to a low speed and gradually add the flour mixture. Divide the dough in half. Put each half in plastic wrap and chill it in the refrigerator for at least one hour. Heat oven to 350° F (180° C). On a floured surface, roll dough to $^1/_8$ inch (0.3 cm) thick. Cut out star shapes with cookie cutters. Put the stars on a baking sheet and refrigerate them for about 15 minutes, until the dough is firm. Bake 8 to 10 minutes, or until crisp. After the cookies cool, decorate them with icing and sprinkles.

# How to make
# Marzipan* Critters

**You will need:**
- large bowl
- I pound (450 g) almond paste*
- $1/3$ cup (80 ml) light corn syrup
- I teaspoon vanilla extract
- I cup (240 ml) marshmallow cream
- wooden spoon
- 6 cups (660 g) powdered sugar
- food coloring
- plastic wrap

**❶** In a large bowl, mix together the almond paste, light corn syrup, vanilla extract, and marshmallow cream. Blend well, using a wooden spoon.

**❷** Add powdered sugar, a little at a time, being sure to blend the sugar in completely each time before adding more. Keep blending in more powdered sugar until the marzipan is firm enough to hold its shape.

**❸** Decide how many colors you want to use and divide the marzipan into that number of balls. Mix a few drops of food coloring into each ball. **Knead** each marzipan ball until it is smooth, then put each ball in plastic wrap. Let the balls sit for 24 hours. Now you're ready to shape marzipan critters!

 Marzipan that is ready for coloring and shaping can usually be found in stores around Christmas and Easter. If you can't find it ready-made, or to use marzipan at other times of the year, just follow this recipe to make your own from almond paste. Tubes of almond paste are sold at grocery stores, with the baking supplies.

# INDIA

**Did You Know?**

Cinnamon comes from the bark of a tree — the cinnamon tree. Originally, cinnamon trees grew only in Sri Lanka, which is an island in the Indian Ocean, off the southern coast of India.

The country of India is very colorful, and so are the many spices used in Indian cuisine. Visiting a spice trader in an Indian marketplace is a feast for the eyes, with mounds of bright yellow tumeric and cumin, brown cloves and coriander, red cayenne pepper, and green cardamom, to name just a few. Curry powder is not one spice but a mixture of spices. The Indian name for curry powder is *garam masala* (gahr-AHM mah-SAH-lah).

Each region in India has its own special foods. In the North, people eat mostly meat and bread. The meat is cooked in underground clay ovens that are called *tandoors* (TAHN-doorz). Farther south, Indian food is spicier, and people eat rice instead of bread with their meals. The people in India's southern regions are mostly Hindu, which is the main religion of India. Hindus are not allowed to eat meat. They eat lots of vegetables and beans. The Indian word for beans is *dal* (dahl). In Indian cooking, dal is a basic ingredient.

## Mangoes

The national fruit of India is the mango. Mangoes come in hundreds of varieties that are different shapes, sizes, and colors.

# How to make **Raita**

**You will need:**
- knife
- cutting board
- vegetable peeler
- small spoon
- 2 bowls
- measuring cups and spoons
- wooden spoon

## Ingredients:

- I tablespoon finely chopped onion
- I ripe tomato, chopped
- I tablespoon chopped fresh cilantro

- I medium cucumber
- I tablespoon salt
- I cup (240 ml) plain yogurt*
- I teaspoon ground cumin

 Have a grown-up prepare the vegetable ingredients for you by chopping the onion, tomato, and cilantro, peeling the cucumber, and slicing it in half lengthwise. With a small spoon, scoop the seeds out of the cucumber and throw them away. Then have a grown-up cut both halves of the cucumber into thin slices. Combine the cucumber, onions, and salt in a bowl. Mix with a wooden spoon and let sit for five minutes. Then squeeze the cucumber and onions to remove the water and transfer them to a dry bowl. Add the tomato and cilantro. Gently stir in the yogurt and cumin, carefully combining all ingredients. Cover and refrigerate for at least one hour before serving. Scooping raita into cucumber boats is a clever serving idea.

 Yogurt is a common ingredient in Indian cooking. It is used in salty recipes as well as sweet ones.

# How to make Mango Lassi

**Ingredients:**

I fresh mango

I cup (240 ml) plain yogurt

I cup (240 ml) cold water

3 ice cubes

4 tablespoons sugar

**You will need:**
- knife
- cutting board
- measuring cups and spoons
- blender
- drinking glass

 Have a grown-up cut open the mango, remove the pit, then peel and chop the mango. Put the chopped mango, yogurt, water, ice cubes, and sugar into a blender. Cover the blender and, holding the lid down securely, blend all of the ingredients for 30 to 45 seconds. Pour the sweet lassi into a drinking glass — and enjoy!

# JAPAN

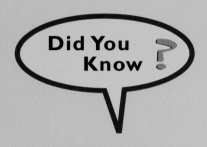

Japanese cooking uses few spices. People in Japan prefer simple foods and fresh flavors.

The Japanese word for meal is *gohan* (goh-HAHN), which means "steamed rice." Rice, however, is more than just food in Japan. It is also used to make paper, fuel, and wine. Rice is so important that the Japanese say the shadow of a full moon looks like a rabbit pounding *o-mochi*, which are gooey rice cakes.

The Japanese also eat noodles. Japanese cooks use three main types of noodles: udon, soba, and ramen. In Japan, making slurping sounds while you are eating noodles is not bad manners because slurping means that you are enjoying the meal.

For meals, the Japanese take great care in decorating the table and arranging the food attractively on plates and in bowls. Because Japanese houses have no chairs, people sit on the floor, on woven grass mats called *tatami* (tah-tah-MEE), and eat at low tables. For special occasions, they wear **kimonos** (kee-MOH-nohs).

# How to use **Hashi***

**①** Hold one chopstick with the thick end down between your thumb and your index finger.

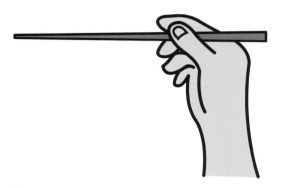

**③** Place the second chopstick between your thumb and your index finger, above the first chopstick.

**②** Rest the thinner, pointed end of the chopstick lightly against your middle finger.

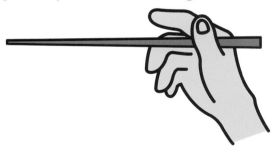

**④** Move the second chopstick up and down, touching the pointed end against the pointed end of the first chopstick. Try not to move the first chopstick.

*Hashi* (HAH-shee) is what Japanese people call chopsticks. The Japanese use large chopsticks as cooking utensils and small, pointed chopsticks to eat their food — even soup with noodles!

# How to make a

# Nori Sushi Roll

**You will need:**
- vinegar
- nori (dried seaweed sheets, available at Asian food stores)
- makisu (bamboo mat) or dish towel
- 1 cup (100 g) sushi rice
- cucumbers and carrots, sliced to look like matchsticks
- plastic wrap
- sharp knife
- damp cloth

**❶** Wet your hands with vinegar to keep the food from sticking.

**❷** Place one sheet of nori on the makisu.

**❸** Spread sushi rice on the nori, leaving a 2-inch (5-cm) bare spot at the end farthest from you and a $^1/_3$-inch (1-cm) bare spot at the end closest to you. Place the cucumbers and carrots on top of the rice about 2 inches (5 cm) from the end closest to you.

**❹** Lift the makisu to begin rolling the nori. As you roll, press the fillings in firmly so they stay in place. With the flat of your hand on the makisu, push the roll forward and backward several times.

**❺** Wrap the sushi roll in plastic. Before serving, have a grown-up slice the roll into circles, using a damp cloth to keep the blade of the knife clean.

# How to make
# Sushi Rice

**Ingredients:**
$^1/_4$ cup (60 ml) rice vinegar
2 tablespoons sugar
1 teaspoon salt
2 cups (400 g) rice
2 cups (480 ml) water

**You will need:**
- measuring cups and spoons
- glass bowl
- wooden spoon
- covered saucepan
- large, flat container

Measure the rice vinegar into a glass bowl. Stir in the sugar and the salt. Put the rice and the water in a saucepan. Heat it on the stove until the water boils, then cover the pan and let the rice **simmer** for about 20 minutes. Take the rice off the heat. Let it stand for about 10 minutes. Empty the cooked rice into a large, flat container. Slowly sprinkle the vinegar mixture over the rice, **folding** it in gently.

# MEXICO

**Did You Know?**

The Spanish name for the fruit of the prickly pear cactus is *tuna*! Although this popular Mexican fruit has very sharp thorns, it tastes as sweet as kiwifruit.

Tortillas (tor-TEE-yahs) are round, flat pancakes made out of ground corn. Mexicans love them! They eat tortillas like bread, plain or in soups or rolled around meats, beans, cheeses, or chili sauces. At every meal, Mexicans eat at least one of three national foods — tortillas, beans, and chilies.

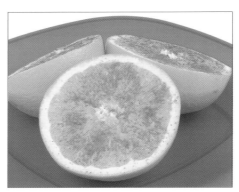

Mexican cooking uses over a hundred varieties of chilies. In some parts of Mexico, oranges cut in half and sprinkled with chili pepper are a popular snack food!

Along with chilies and many other spices, Mexico is where cacao (kah-KAH-oh) was first grown. Chocolate is made from cacao beans. In **precolonial** days, the cacao bean was a highly prized food. Chocolate is still an important part of many Mexican dishes, but it is not always sweet. *Mole* (MOH-lay) is spicy chocolate sauce commonly served hot over chicken. In Mexico, chocolate-flavored dishes top the list of children's favorite foods, followed by quesadillas (kay-sah-DEE-yass), tacos, and burritos.

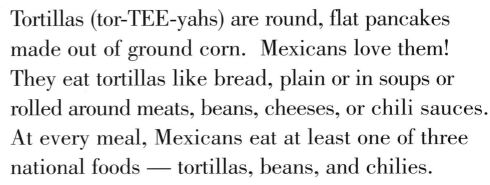

# How to make Tacos*

**Ingredients:**

| | |
|---|---|
| 1 pound (450 g) ground beef | chopped lettuce |
| 1 packet of taco seasoning | chopped tomatoes |
| $^2/_3$ cup (160 ml) water | chopped green onions |
| taco shells | salsa |
| 1 can of refried beans | sour cream |
| shredded cheddar cheese | |

**You will need:**
- large saucepan
- measuring cup
- can opener
- spoons and bowls
- knife
- cutting board

Have a grown-up cook the ground beef in a saucepan with the taco seasoning and water, following the directions on the seasoning packet. A grown-up should also help you warm the taco shells in the oven, at 350° F (180° C) for about 10 minutes. Open the can of beans and spoon them into a serving bowl.

Put the shredded cheese in a separate serving bowl. Have a grown-up chop the lettuce, tomatoes, and onions. Put each of these taco toppings in a separate bowl with a serving spoon, where necessary. Fill a taco shell by starting with meat or beans, then adding cheese and your choice of vegetables. Top the taco with salsa or sour cream.

The Spanish word *taco* actually means "snack," but, today, the word is used for one dish in particular — a sandwich in a tortilla. Tortillas that are already fried and folded over are sold as "taco shells" in grocery stores.

# RUSSIA

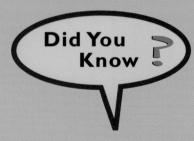

No matter what time of day or night, guests in Russian homes are always invited to share a meal. **Hospitality** is very important in Russia. Because the country has such long, cold winters, Russians like to eat hearty soups such as *borscht* (BORSHT), which is a red beet soup, and *shchi* (SHEE), which is cabbage soup.

For children in Russia, pastries filled with chopped cabbage and meat are a favorite food. Children also love *blinis* (BLEE-nees), which are little pancakes. Russians will make a meal of these pancakes for lunch or dinner. Although blinis are eaten all year round, they are made, traditionally, on Shrovetide, which is the last day of winter and the first day of spring. In Russia, the end of a cold winter is a time for celebrating. Children often decorate their homes with brightly colored paper chains and paper lanterns.

## Samovars

Because Russians love to drink black tea, every house, office, factory, and even train car has a samovar (SA-muh-vahr). A samovar is a huge urn filled with water that is kept hot either by electricity or by a tube inside it that is filled with burning charcoal. On top of the samovar sits a small teapot of strong tea. The teapot is continually refilled with the hot water from the samovar.

# How to make **Paper Lanterns***

**You will need:**
- **sheets of paper in many different colors**
- **scissors**
- **tape or glue**

**❶** Fold each sheet of paper in half. Make cuts along the folded edge to about two-thirds of the way across the paper.

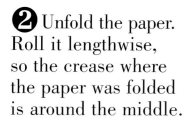

**❷** Unfold the paper. Roll it lengthwise, so the crease where the paper was folded is around the middle.

**❸** Tape or glue the long sides of the rolled paper. Cut a small strip of paper and glue it at the top for a handle.

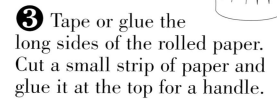

If you are going to have a blinis party, you will want to decorate the room with colorful Russian paper lanterns! Glue on glitter or sequins or draw designs on the paper with crayons or markers to make your lanterns even more festive.

# How to make **Blinis**

## Ingredients:

2 eggs

2 cups (480 ml) milk

$\frac{1}{2}$ teaspoon salt

1 cup (150 g)
  unbleached flour

$\frac{1}{2}$ teaspoon baking soda

2 tablespoons vegetable oil

sour cream

jam

**You will need:**
- measuring cups and spoons
- mixing bowl
- wooden spoon
- frying pan
- spatula

 Combine the eggs and the milk in a mixing bowl. Add the salt, flour, and baking soda. Stir well to remove all lumps. Have a grown-up pour vegetable oil into a frying pan and heat it on medium high. Pour $\frac{1}{4}$ cup (60 ml) of blini batter into the oil.

When bubbles appear on the surface (after about 2 minutes), flip the blini with a spatula and cook the other side to a golden color (about 2 more minutes). Remove the blini from the frying pan and make some more. Top each blini with a tablespoon of sour cream and a teaspoon of jam. Serve and enjoy!

# SOUTH AFRICA

South Africa is often called the Rainbow Country because of its many different cultures, languages, and religions. South African cuisine is also an interesting mix of East, West, North, and South, blending spices and flavors from Africa, Asia, and Europe. South Africans cook a traditional European dish that is like a chicken pot pie, but they add ingredients such as raisins, almonds, and apples and spice it up with curry powder. *Blatjang* (BLUD-chang), which is **chutney**, and *atjar* (UT-char), which are pickles, are Indian **condiments** that are served with most South African meals.

Children growing up in South Africa are treated to the natural bounty of the country's land and oceans. They enjoy the fresh tropical flavors of the fruits and vegetables that flourish in the mild climate, and because South Africa is bordered by two oceans, the Atlantic and the Indian, fish and seafood are part of everyone's diet.

## The Baobob

If you stand on your head, a baobab (BAY-uh-bab) tree won't look upside down! The baobob has a very thick trunk, up to 50 feet (15 m) around, and its branches look like roots. This tree can live up to a thousand years. Mixed with water or milk, the pulp inside the baobob's fruit makes a cool drink.

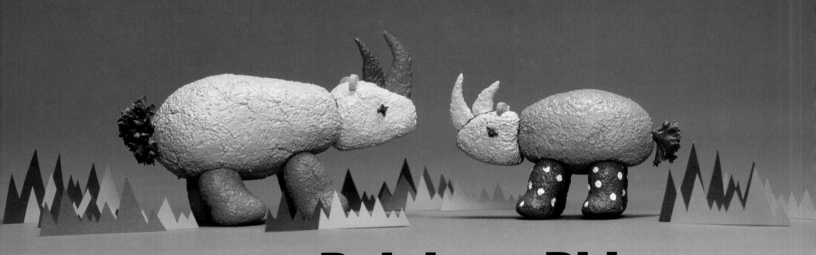

# How to make a Rainbow Rhino

**You will need:**
- medium-size bowl
- large spoon
- measuring cups
- $^{1}/_{4}$ cup (38 g) flour
- $^{1}/_{2}$ cup (90 g) uncooked grits*
- $^{1}/_{4}$ cup (60 ml) water
- acrylic paints
- paintbrush
- toothpicks
- cloves
- parsley
- carrot slices

❶ In a medium-size bowl, combine the flour and the grits, then stir in the water. Mix well to make dough.

❷ Roll a large amount of dough between your hands to form the body of a rhinoceros. Use a smaller amount of dough to make the rhino's head. Use equal amounts of dough to make legs. Form more dough into two cone-shaped horns. One horn should be longer than the other.

❸ Let the dough shapes dry overnight. When they are dry, paint each shape a different color.

❹ When the paint on all the shapes is dry, put the rhinoceros together, using toothpicks to attach the parts. Add cloves for eyes and a sprig of parsley for a tail. Have a grown-up cut a carrot slice in half for ears.

 In South Africa, grits called *pap* are a popular side dish with many meals.

# How to make Fish Fingers

### Ingredients:

1 pound (450 g) whitefish, skinned and boned

$^1/_2$ cup (75 g) flour

2 eggs

6 to 7 ounces (170 to 200 g) plain corn chips, tortilla chips, or cornflakes cereal

vegetable cooking spray

tartar sauce

**You will need:**
- knife
- cutting board
- measuring cups
- 3 mixing bowls
- wooden spoon
- plastic bag
- rolling pin
- baking sheet

Have a grown-up heat the oven to 400° F (200° C) and cut the fish into finger-length strips. Put the flour in a shallow bowl. Beat eggs lightly with a wooden spoon in separate small bowl. Put the corn chips, tortilla chips, or cornflakes in a plastic bag and crush them lightly with a rolling pin. Pour the crumbs into another bowl.

Coat each strip of fish with flour. Dip the floured fish strips into the eggs, then roll them in the crumbs. Arrange the fish fingers on a baking sheet, spray them lightly with vegetable cooking spray, and bake them for 15 to 20 minutes or until crisp and golden. Serve with tartar sauce.

# UNITED STATES

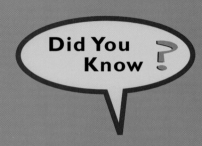
Pizza, french fries, hotdogs, peanut butter and jelly, and macaroni and cheese are favorite foods of all American children, but the United States is a big country with different growing seasons and a variety of traditions. Children in the Northeast like to pick blueberries and make blueberry pancakes to eat drenched with maple syrup. Children in the South love watermelon. Children in the Midwest enjoy corn on the cob every summer.

Popcorn is probably the most original American food. Native Americans made popcorn long before Europeans first arrived on the continent. Most of the world's popcorn is grown in Nebraska and Indiana.

For special events and on many holidays, especially Christmas and Thanksgiving, families in the United States gather to enjoy each other's company and to share a feast, which often includes turkey, stuffing, cranberry sauce, and pumpkin pie.

## Popsicles

Who invented Popsicles? It was eleven-year-old Frank Epperson. In 1905, Epperson stirred a soft drink with a stick and, by mistake, left it on the back porch overnight. The soda pop froze with the stick in it. Years later, Epperson sold these frozen treats. He called them "Epsicles."

# How to make a
# Macaroni Mosaic

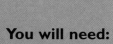

**You will need:**
- food coloring
- water
- 4 or more paper cups,
  12-ounce (360 ml) size
  or larger
- 2 cups (280 g) macaroni,
  in different shapes and sizes
- spoon
- paper towel
- heavy paper or cardboard
- glue

**1** Mix a few drops of food coloring with water in a paper cup. You can also mix two colors, such as blue and yellow to make green.

**2** Put some macaroni in the cup and stir it until all of the pieces are colored. Lay the macaroni on a paper towel to dry.

**3** Repeat steps 1 and 2 to make at least four different colors of macaroni.

**4** When the macaroni is dry, arrange it in a design on a piece of heavy paper or cardboard and glue it in place.

# How to make S'mores

**You will need:**
- marshmallows
- long barbecue fork or a straightened wire hanger
- campfire
- graham crackers
- chocolate bars

American children love to camp out and roast marshmallows over an open fire. S'mores are a campfire tradition. The name came from how good they taste — children always ask for "s'more."

**❶** Put a marshmallow on the end of a long fork or a straightened-out wire hanger and roast it over a fire until it is lightly browned. If you don't have a campfire, you can roast your marshmallow on a plate in a microwave oven for 30 seconds.

**❷** Place the gooey marshmallow on a graham cracker.

**❸** Put a piece of a chocolate bar on top of the marshmallow. Put another graham cracker on top of the chocolate. Mash the top graham cracker down lightly to spread out the marshmallow. After you eat one of these tasty treats, you'll ask for s'more!

# Glossary

**Aborigines:** the earliest inhabitants of Australia

**chickpeas:** the round, beanlike seeds of a plant that is grown for food in India and the Middle East

**chutney:** an Indian sauce that is made from a mixture of fruit, vinegar, sugar, and spices

**colonized:** settled a new land

**condiments:** seasonings and other food items that add flavor to a meal

**cuisine:** the foods of a particular country or region or the way those foods are prepared

**dumplings:** lumps of seasoned dough that are usually steamed and served in soups or stews

**equator:** the hot, damp region around the center of Earth that gets direct sunlight all year round.

**extinct:** no longer in existence

**folding:** combining ingredients by gently turning them over and over

**grub:** the thick, wormlike larva of certain insects, such as beetles

**hospitality:** the kind treatment a host gives his or her guests

**kimonos:** loose robes with wide sleeves and a sash, traditionally worn by Japanese women

**knead:** to press, fold, and stretch dough with the hands

**precolonial:** related to the time before a land or region was colonized

**predator:** an animal that hunts and kills other animals, usually for food

**rationing:** the practice of controlling the amounts of food and other items people can buy when supplies are low, such as during wars or famines

**simmer:** cook gently in boiling water

**skewered:** pierced with a thin stick of wood or metal to hold it in place for cooking

**slang:** words or expressions that are common to a language or group of people but are not standard usage

**spatula:** a kitchen utensil with a broad, flat blade at one end that is used to remove food from pans

# More Books to Read

*Around the World with Food & Spices* (series). Melinda Lilly (Rourke)

*Food. Around the World* (series). Margaret C. Hall (Heinemann Library)

*Food and Recipes of Africa*. Theresa M. Beatty (PowerKids Press)

*Food and Recipes of Japan*. Theresa M. Beatty (PowerKids Press)

*Food and Recipes of Mexico*. Theresa M. Beatty (PowerKids Press)

*It's Disgusting and We Ate It! True Food Facts from Around the World and Throughout History*. James Solheim (Simon & Schuster)

*Kids Around the World Cook! The Best Foods and Recipes from Many Lands*. Arlette N. Braman (Econo-Clad Books)

*The Kids' Around the World Cookbook*. Deri Robins (Econo-Clad Books)

*A Taste of India. Food Around the World* (series). Roz Denny (Raintree/Steck-Vaughn)

# Web Sites

*The Edible Journey through China*
library.thinkquest.org/C0122155/

*Japanese Cookbook for Kids*
www.jinjapan.org/kidsweb/cook/intro/intro.html

*Kids Kings of the Kitchen*
www.scoreone.com/kids_kitchen

*Peace Corps Kids World Food, Friends, and Fun: Food in Russia*
www.peacecorps.gov/kids/like/russia-food.html

*Really Cookin': Kids' Recipe Features*
www2.whirlpool.com/html/homelife/cookin/morekrec.htm

# Index

Chantrell Creek Elementary